Bill & Ben

Tricky Sticky Stuff

BBC

One afternoon, The Man Who Worked in the Garden was busy in the shed. He was making a great deal of noise.

As soon as he left, Bill and Ben hopped down from their flowerpots. *"Flobadobalop!"* said Bill. *"Flubadubadook!"* said Ben. They wanted to see what The Man had been doing in the shed.

"Be careful," said Weed. "Don't let The Man find you, he may not be away for very long."
Bill and Ben quickly climbed up to the top of the workbench ... and stopped in surprise.

"Aw, flobadobolob!" said Bill.

In the middle of the bench was a statue.
"*Oooh! Flubadubading*," said Ben.

They walked all round it. Then Ben reached
out and touched the statue's head.

Suddenly, the head fell right off and bounced across the workbench.

"*Flubadubalub!*" said Ben, running forward.

It teetered on the edge of the workbench...

Ben dived to catch it, "*Oooopht!*"

The head slipped from his grasp, spun up into the air and fell...

PLOP!

...into a pot of paint.

"*Flobadob!*" said Bill. What were they going to do now?

Bill and Ben went to find something to mend the statue.
But first, they met Pry, the magpie. She was in trouble, too,
with a roll of sticky tape stuck to her beak.
"*Flobalob?*" asked Bill.

"I found this shiny
plastic thing," Pry
mumbled, "but it's
full of sticky stuff
and I can't get it off!"

Ben took hold of the
sticky tape and pulled.
"*Flub!*"
Pry was free! "Ooo,
thank you!" she said,
very relieved.

Bill looked at the sticky stuff and, *"**Flobalob!**"*, he had an idea. They could use the sticky tape to mend things … and it might even mend the statue!

Hurrying back to the shed, Bill and Ben met Scamper, the squirrel. She was holding two halves of a large walnut in her paws.

"I've been saving this nut for a special day!" said Scamper. "But now the shell's broken in two. What shall I do?"

*"**Flobalob!**"* said Bill, who'd had another idea.
*"**Flubaticky!**"* said Ben. They could use the sticky stuff!

Bill took Scamper's nut and wound the sticky
tape all around it.
"Oh, that's brilliant!" said Scamper. "Thank you!
When it really is a special day I'll … I'll …
I'll let you watch me eat it!"

But Bill and Ben didn't think very much of that.

Bill and Ben were in even more of a hurry now. They ran so fast, they didn't see Slowcoach, the tortoise, and fell right over him.

"Dear me!" he said. "Why all the hurry?"
"*Robaflobadend!*" said Bill.

"You have to mend something? I wish I could mend my map of the garden," said Slowcoach, sadly. "It's so old, it's ripped in two. Of course, you're in a hurry. No time to help old friends…"

"*Aw, flubalub, Slobalob*," said Ben.

Bill and Ben followed Slowcoach into his house. Quickly, Bill mended the map with the sticky tape, and they scooted away before Slowcoach could keep them any longer.

Bill skidded to a stop outside the shed – but where had Ben got to? Just then, Boo, the hedgehog, rolled past. Bill asked him if he had seen Ben.

"Oh yes," said Boo. "I saw him here … last Thursday. The next day, I saw him there… And today … I saw him over there talking to Tad."

"*Flobadobalob!*" muttered Bill, and rushed over to join them.

"It's that Rose," Tad, the frog, was saying. "Keeps going on at me to stick her leaf back on. Any ideas?"

Ben held up the sticky tape. "*Flubadub!*" he said.

But Bill thought they should go and mend the statue.

"Aah … Rose would give you a *reward*," said Tad carefully.

"*Aw, robadubadord!*" And off they zoomed to see Rose.

"Careful," said Rose, as Bill and Ben began to mend her leaf. "I'm terribly ticklish… Oh! Hee, hee, hee!" she giggled.

"*Robadob!*" said Bill, when they'd finished. "That was quick," said Rose.

Ben held out his hand. *"Rubadubadord?"*
"Oh yes, you may have a reward," said Rose.
"You may sniff my wonderful scent!"

"Flub!" said Ben, pulling a face.
Who wants to sniff a smelly rose?

They didn't want The Man to catch them,
so Bill and Ben hurried to the shed.
"What have you two got there?" asked Thistle.
"*Flobadobalobadob*," said Bill.

"Sticky stuff, is it? For mending things?"
purred Thistle. "Oh, I might be able to help."

She began to give Bill and Ben instructions. Bill and Ben did what she said and walked backwards, struggling with the sticky tape. Soon it was wrapped all round them.

"You're STUCK!" cried Thistle. She laughed and laughed – until she was covered in sticky tape, too!

Bill and Ben staggered about the garden trying to free themselves.

"*Flobalobaduck!*" said Bill when they reached Weed.
"Well, I can see you're stuck!" said Weed. "Stand still and
do just as I say…"

They did exactly as Weed told them … and soon they were both free.

"*Flubadubaleed!*" said Ben.

"*Aw, robalub!*" said Bill.

Then Bill remembered they still had to mend the statue.

"*Aw, flobadobalob!*" he gasped, and they both raced away to the shed.

They rescued the head
from the pot of paint, and
Ben stuck it on the statue
with the sticky tape.

"*Aw! Haw, haw, flobadob!*"
laughed Bill. The head was
back to front! Ben stepped back crossly
and put his foot into a puddle of sticky stuff.
"*Errr … flubaticky*," said Ben. He'd
landed on a tube of glue!

"Aww ... uffff ... ohhh!"
Bill heaved and pulled at Ben.
Suddenly, he came unstuck
and shot right over
Bill's head!

Then Bill had an idea.
"Robadobadend!"
He put some of the glue on
the neck of the statue, and Ben
stuck the head on top. The
statue was mended!

And just then they heard The
Man opening the shed door...

"*Flubalub!*" gasped Ben.
Then, "*Flobadide*," they both whispered

Ben dived under
a piece of cloth
on the workbench...

...and Bill hid behind some
flowerpots on the shelf.

They had to stay hidden, shivering and shaking, the whole time The Man was working in the shed.

They were there for ages, and it was almost dark when they made their way wearily back home and tumbled into their pots.

"Hello, Bill. Hello, Ben," called
Weed. "What took you so long?"
But they each gave one big,
stretchy, sleepy yawn … and fell
back into their pots, asleep.
"Never mind," smiled Weed.
"Tell me tomorrow."

The End